WITHDRAWN

ALEXANDRIA PUBLIC LIBRARY
10 Maple Drive - Box 357
Alexandria, Ohio 43001

SOUTH AFRICA

by
Gail B. Stewart

CRESTWOOD HOUSE
New York

Collier Macmillan Canada
Toronto

Maxwell Macmillan International Publishing Group
New York Oxford Singapore Sydney

Library of Congress Cataloging-in-Publication Data
Stewart, Gail, 1949-
  South Africa/by Gail B. Stewart. — 1st ed.
    p. cm. — (Places in the news)
  Summary: Examines historical and recent events that have kept South Africa in the news.
  ISBN 0-89686-539-8
    1. Apartheid—South Africa—Juvenile litcrature. 2. South Africa—History—Juvenile literature. [1. Apartheid—South Africa. 2. South Africa—History.] I. Title. II. Series: Stewart, Gail, 1949- Places in the news.
  DT1757.S74   1990
  968—dc20   90-36292
                                                                                                    CIP
                                                                                                    AC

Photo Credits
Cover: Magnum Photos, Inc.: (Gideon Mendel)
Magnum Photos, Inc.: (Gideon Mendel) 4, 20, 26, 29; (ian Berry) 10, 13, 16, 42; (C. Steele) 23, 35
AP—Wide World Photos: 32, 38

Copyright © 1990 Crestwood House, Macmillan Publishing Company

All rights reserved. No part of this book may be reproduced or transmitted in any form or by any means, electronic or mechanical, including photocopying, recording, or by any information storage and retrieval system, without permission in writing from the Publisher.

Macmillan Publishing Company
866 Third Avenue
New York, NY 10022

Collier Macmillan Canada, Inc.
1200 Eglinton Avenue East
Suite 200
Don Mills, Ontario M3C 3N1

Produced by Flying Fish Studio Incorporated

Printed in the United States of America

First Edition

10 9 8 7 6 5 4 3 2 1

CONTENTS

South Africa in the News...5

The Roots of Apartheid..8

The System of Apartheid...14

Fighting Apartheid...24

South Africa and the World..36

Facts about South Africa...44

Glossary..45

Index...46

SOUTH AFRICA IN THE NEWS

September 6, 1989, was Election Day in South Africa. The nation's president had recently stepped down. The acting president, Frederik de Klerk, had not been officially chosen. De Klerk had to be approved by South Africa's lawmaking body, Parliament. Voters had to choose their representatives for Parliament.

But this day was not a day of celebration for South Africa. Instead, Election Day resulted in riots, protests, and bloodshed. When the day was over, 29 people had been killed in the violence. More than 300 people had been treated for injuries.

All of the deaths and injuries were among South Africa's black and colored (mixed race) people. More than three million of them had stayed home from work on Election Day. They did this to protest the fact that they aren't allowed to vote. Only whites in South Africa are permitted to vote.

Many of the people who stayed home from work on September 6 went to rallies and demonstrations. Some people marched with large signs that carried anti-government slogans. Most black

On Election Day in 1989 many blacks in South Africa held demonstrations to demand the right to vote. Currently only whites can vote.

and colored South Africans live in areas called townships outside the cities. Police were sent to the townships by the government to control the crowds.

However, the police did more than control the crowds. Many witnesses, including some police, said that the police behaved like "wild dogs." Clothed in riot gear, they ran through the streets of nine different townships, carrying whips, shotguns, and tear-gas canisters. Witnesses reported that the police fired at random down streets and into crowds.

Some of those killed or injured were taking part in the Election Day protests. However, many were merely bystanders. One 13-year-old boy was on his way to buy a book at a store when a police van rounded the corner and fired at him. He was shot in the head and badly wounded.

Another victim was a five-year-old girl. She had been startled by the sounds of the shooting, witnesses said. As she tried to run to a safe place, she was hit in the stomach by a stray bullet. No doctors were nearby during the violence, and so she bled to death.

One policeman admitted that groups of officers chased crowds of black and colored people, lashing at them with whips and firing at them with shotguns. Government officials declared Election Day 1989 the bloodiest in the country's history.

In many countries around the world, an election would be a chance for citizens to be heard. Elections are a time when people show how they want their nation to be governed. This was certainly not the case in South Africa.

Most of South Africa's population is not permitted to vote. In fact, of the nation's 37 million people, less than 5 million are

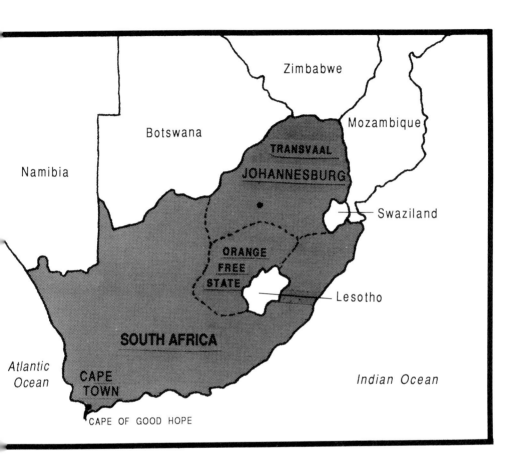

allowed to vote! These 5 million are the white people of South Africa.

South Africa is one of the only places on earth where such a tiny minority of people still controls a large majority of the population. There are 3 million colored people and 1 million Asians in South Africa. The largest segment of the people—more than 28 million—is black.

However, the white population controls almost every aspect of life in South Africa. The white government makes the decisions about housing, education, and jobs. The white government controls who has power and who does not.

How is it possible for such a small minority to control such a large majority? South Africa has a system of laws organized to keep power in the hands of the white people. This system is called apartheid. In Afrikaans, the language of the ruling class, "apartheid" means "apartness." Afrikaans is a mixture of English, Dutch, and a variety of African languages. Being apart, or segregated, is the whole idea behind the system.

The system of apartheid was officially adopted by South Africa in 1948. However, the beginnings of apartheid go back much further, to the arrival of the Dutch in South Africa in the 17th century.

THE ROOTS OF APARTHEID

Even before the first white people set foot in South Africa, sailors from Europe knew it was there. They often sailed around the southern tip of Africa, called the Cape of Good Hope. These sailors were looking for the easiest water route to India.

The journey from Europe to India was a long, dangerous one. Sailors would welcome a supply of fresh water and good food along the way. The Dutch set up a business on the cape to provide these things to the sailors. They called this business the Dutch East India Company.

Slavery in South Africa

The Dutch were a strict and very religious group of people. In many ways, they were similar to the Puritans who lived in America in the 17th century. The Dutch believed that white people were superior to blacks. The source of this idea, they said, was the Bible. Therefore, they believed it was not wrong to use black Africans as slaves. These slaves did most of the heavy, dirty work in the Dutch community.

By the end of the 17th century, a new racial group had begun in South Africa. Today they are called coloreds; they were the children of black African women and white Dutchmen.

The Boers

Some of the Dutch were more adventurous and independent than others. These people decided to go off on their own. Hoping to discover new sites for their farms, these "Boers" (the Dutch word for farmers) left the cape area and settled in the lands just to the north.

In the late 18th century, the British took over the Cape of Good

Hope. They were a mighty world power then and had no trouble claiming the land as their own. However, as the British began settling in South Africa, they brought their own rules. One of the most important changes they made was to abolish slavery.

The Boers were a very independent group of people. They had no intention of changing their ways because of British rule. They moved even farther north, and east, eventually settling in what is now called the Orange Free State and Transvaal. As long as they were far from the cape and British rule, they believed they could do as they pleased.

The Chosen People

As they made their way north, the Boers thought of themselves as God's chosen people. They compared themselves to the Hebrews of the Old Testament. In the Bible, the Hebrews were God's chosen people. God would remind the Hebrews of how special they were by showing them signs and wonders along the way.

The Boers claim that God showed them such a sign on their journey. The Boers encountered a huge tribe of Zulu warriors. The Zulus, armed with spears, wanted to fight. They intended to drive out the white intruders. Ten thousand Zulus, on a cue from their chief, rushed at the group of covered wagons. The Boers waited, muskets ready.

As the story goes, only three of the Boers were killed in the attack. Although they were greatly outnumbered, the Boers killed three thousand Zulus in an afternoon. The ground was covered with their bodies. Their blood poured into a nearby river (later

South Africa first became important to European sailors, who stopped at the Cape of Good Hope on the way to India.

named Blood River). This, thought the Boers, was the sign that God was on their side. They were God's chosen people.

Changing Hands

The British might never have gone into the Boer territory if it hadn't been for a young boy named Erasmus Jacob. The son of one of the Boers, Erasmus found a sparkling pebble one day. It turned out to be a huge diamond, worth a fortune. The Boers soon discovered many diamonds in this place, which was later called Kimberley. Soon hundreds of people poured into the area, all wanting to become rich.

The British were interested, too. They claimed the area, but the Boers refused to hand it over. A war began between the British and the Boers, called the Boer War. It was a long and bloody struggle, lasting from 1899 to 1902. By the time it was finally won by the British, more than 22,000 British soldiers had died. Some 6,000 Boers had died in battle; another 26,000 Boer women and children had died in British concentration camps.

Even though the Boers had lost the war, they soon regained control of the country. Eight years later, the British made South Africa part of the British empire and gave the Boers self-rule. It wasn't until 1931 that South Africa became fully independent.

Under the constitution of the new country, whites had total power. Of the two groups of whites, the Boers—or Afrikaners, as they came to be called—outnumbered the British. They claimed political power for themselves. As time went by, the Afrikaners tightened their control over the black, Asian, and colored people.

Diamond mining, which is still a big industry in South Africa, was the cause of the Boer War in 1899. Both the Dutch and the English wanted to control this powerful business.

THE SYSTEM OF APARTHEID

While the British South Africans were fairly tolerant—or liberal—toward the black and colored populations, the Afrikaners were set against mingling with them.

The Afrikaners were very conservative, or reluctant to change. They thought of themselves as children of the "chosen people"—the Boers who had conquered many of the black tribes of Africa. The Afrikaners believed that they were superior to other races, especially the blacks. They thought of themselves as adults and of the blacks as children who needed guidance. This kind of thinking is called racial supremacy—in this case, white supremacy.

Apartheid Begins

When South Africa became independent in 1931, the leaders of the Afrikaners tried to unify the whites. It was important, they believed, for the whites to stick together. Since they were a minority in a mostly black country, they needed to support one another.

However, in 1948 some drastic changes came about. An election in that year brought a man named Daniel Malan to power. Malan was the candidate of the National party. This was a very conservative group of Afrikaners who wanted nothing to do with Britain or its liberal ideas. Malan and his followers had a slogan—"Africa for Afrikaners." Malan was like many other descendants

14

of the Boers. He believed strongly in the idea of white supremacy. He thought there was no room in South Africa for people who thought that the races should be equal.

One of the members of Malan's government was Hendrik Verwoerd. Verwoerd had sided with the Nazis during World War II. Like Hitler, Verwoerd believed that the white race should be kept "pure." Verwoerd designed the apartheid system to keep South Africa's white race pure. The system was set up to keep nonwhites in a low position. If nonwhites were kept powerless, they could be controlled easily by the small minority of whites. Because of this plan, Verwoerd has been called the architect of apartheid.

300 Laws and a Pencil Test

The system of apartheid is actually a series of three hundred separate laws. These laws cover everything from housing and education to marriage and voting. However, the first and most important part of the apartheid system is the Race Classification Act. This law calls for the South African people to be divided into four groups: white, Asian, colored, and black. Each person's classification, or group, is written down in a government record.

In deciding what group a person belongs to, the government looks at several things. Physical appearance is important. So are language and one's ancestors. However, in some cases, a person's appearance can be deceiving. Some whites have been classified as coloreds because their hair is tightly curled or because their

South Africa's apartheid system has separated blacks from whites for many years. Even campgrounds have been divided so that the races cannot mix.

complexion is dark. Sometimes, too, colored people have such light skin and fair hair that they have been labeled white.

Because whites have far more power than colored people, many colored people have tried to convince the government that they are white. When there is a disagreement about what race a person belongs to, a government judge makes the decision. At one time, there was a judge who used to stick a pencil in the person's hair. If the pencil remained in place without slipping, the judge ordered the person classified as colored. Only colored and black people, the judge ruled, had hair coarse enough to hold up a pencil!

"Temporary Dwellers"

Under apartheid, black Africans were not considered citizens of South Africa. Instead, they were thought of as "temporary dwellers." The whites did not want blacks living near them—or even in the same cities or towns.

So instead of giving them citizenship, the government gave the blacks their own separate lands. Called homelands, these areas are far from the settlements and cities of the whites. The home-lands were chosen at random. In other words, no special thought was given to which tribe was placed where. Furthermore, the homelands make up only 13 percent of the total land of South Africa. More than 28 million people originally were assigned to the homelands. The other 87 percent of the land was reserved for 5 million whites!

Ten of these homelands were set up. More than 12 million blacks were eventually moved to the homelands. Then, beginning in 1960, 3.5 million more black people were ordered out of their homes. They were forcibly moved to the homelands.

The quality of the homelands is quite poor. They are usually the dustiest, driest areas. The soil is unfit for growing good crops. A black leader and opponent of apartheid, Archbishop Desmond Tutu, has spoken against the system of homelands. He has called them "dumping places for the people South African whites have no use for."

Townships

Even though the whites wanted little contact with the blacks, the whites depended upon them to do menial work. They wanted them to work on the farms and in the mines. Blacks were used to do low-paying, heavy jobs such as janitor work, garbage collecting, and dishwashing in restaurants.

If all blacks were to live far away on the homelands, however, they could not do these jobs. The government had to set up in-between areas for black workers. These areas, called townships, are located on the outskirts of every town and city in South Africa.

For the many blacks who cannot earn a living in the homelands, the townships are places to live while working in the white towns and cities. Many black South African families are split. The father works and lives in a township, while the rest of the family lives in a homeland. In recent years, however, entire families have settled in the townships.

Soweto is a township near the large city of Johannesburg, or "Joburg," as South Africans have nicknamed it. Joburg has a

18

population of almost 1.5 million. The black township of Soweto has even more people—more than 2 million.

Soweto, which is short for Southwestern Townships, is made up of 100,000 dreary barracks. They are built in rows, of wood and brick. Most have roofs of metal. The houses are very small, with few windows. Each house is crowded. Often 12 to 15 people are crammed into one tiny dwelling.

There is almost no indoor plumbing in Soweto. In many of the houses, there is no electricity either. Gangs of bored or restless teenagers are always a threat, and crime is not unusual. Garbage is not picked up regularly, and it often litters the streets.

People who live in Soweto usually ride to work on a train. The trip to Johannesburg takes about one hour each way, and the train is hot and dirty. There are never enough seats, and many people stand for the entire trip, some after working all day in the city.

There are very few pleasures in the township of Soweto. One of the most popular relaxations is a visit to the swimming pool. In Soweto, a township of 2 million people, there are seven swimming pools. By comparison, there are 25,000 homes with private swimming pools for Johannesburg's white population of 1.5 million.

The Pass Laws

Perhaps the most hated laws of the apartheid system were the pass laws. Until very recently, each black South African had to carry a little brown plastic book at all times. This book was much

The government of South Africa has created townships outside of every city, where blacks who work in the cities are forced to live. These areas are often the scenes of protests and violence.

like a passport. It had a photograph of the person, as well as information about where the person was permitted to live. No black could live anywhere other than a homeland without government permission. And by law, every black had to carry a pass book at all times.

If blacks were stopped for any reason by the police, they had to show their pass books. If they were not carrying them at the time, the blacks were jailed. Tens of thousands of black South Africans were put in jail every year for this offense.

Education

One group can usually control another more easily if that group can keep the other ignorant and uneducated. So for many years, white South Africans have tried to keep blacks from getting a good education.

Half of the blacks in South Africa have had only four years or less of school. At one time, blacks were not expected to attend school at all. Whites and Asians, on the other hand, had to attend school until they were 16.

Now that the government has set up schools for black children, they are for blacks only. White children go to separate schools. This separation of races is called segregation. The differences between these separate schools were outlined by Hendrik Verwoerd in 1953. He declared that all black children should be schooled in the kind of work they would do. It was foolish, he insisted, to teach them anything other than how to do menial labor.

The kinds of books used in black schools did not help students to have high goals. When black Africans were mentioned, they were shown in a negative way. Black characters were lazy, or dishonest, or uncivilized. The heroes of the stories were always white.

Although some changes in black education have occurred in recent years, there are still severe problems. Schools are still segregated. In black schools, one teacher usually instructs 48 children. In white schools, there is one teacher for every 20 students. The government spends ten times as much on the education of a white child than it does on a black child's.

Apartheid and White South Africa

White people in South Africa benefit from apartheid. They are guaranteed the best places to work and the finest living areas. Because they are the only racial group allowed to vote, they control the government.

However, many whites in cities like Johannesburg live in fear. Some believe that their country cannot stay as it is. Sooner or later, they know, the nonwhites will demand equality. Many are afraid that South Africa is in for a bloody, violent time. They foresee a major black revolt in their country.

For this reason, many Afrikaners have large stockpiles of weapons. A typical wealthy Afrikaner has a supply of 20 or 30 weapons, some of them automatic. His or her house has an electric fence surrounding it and is guarded by a dog.

It would be wrong, however, to think that all white South

Until recently, all blacks in South Africa were forced to carry pass books. These books, which had to be shown on demand, limited the areas where a person could travel.

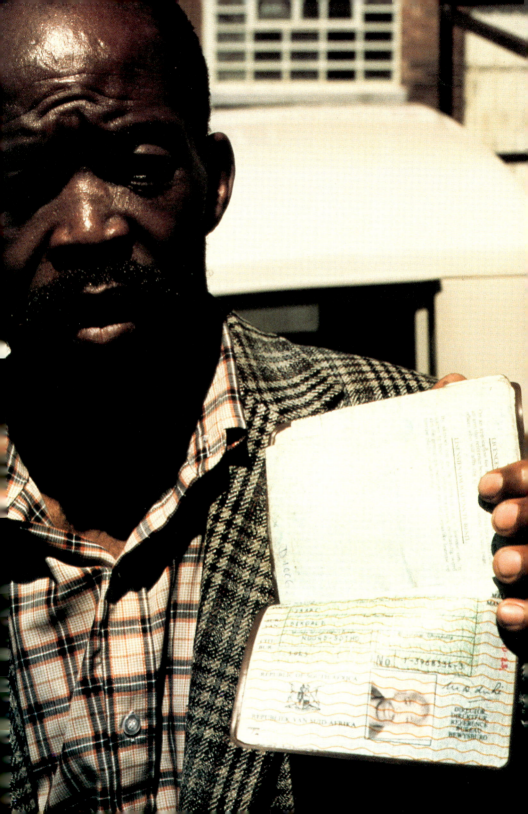

Africans support apartheid and fear violence. That is certainly not the case. Many whites are sympathetic to the way black and colored South Africans have been treated. Rand Llewiston, a 57-year-old mechanic from Johannesburg, is eager for his country to change.

"We cannot grow as a country by standing on the backs of the black people," he says. "Anyone who thinks otherwise is a fool. Their [the blacks'] kids are the future of the country, same as mine."

FIGHTING APARTHEID

You might wonder if black South Africans have ever challenged the white government. The answer is yes, many times. Blacks (and, to a lesser degree, coloreds and Asians) were speaking out against white supremacy even before the apartheid system became official. Their protests continue to this day.

The African National Congress

Even before Daniel Malan and the National party came to power, black South Africans were treated unfairly. There were, however, some educated blacks who tried to change things. These blacks, together with some coloreds and Asians, formed the African National Congress (ANC) in 1912.

The ANC was originally a pacifist organization—it worked in peaceful ways. ANC members talked to government officials and white business owners. They tried to convince the whites that equality would be better for South Africa.

However, the ANC did not accomplish very much. It didn't convince many whites to care about equality for blacks. In the 1950s, the ANC was joined by other groups of blacks who were eager to try different methods of fighting apartheid. They believed more could be accomplished by peacefully resisting and protesting. They thought that strikes and sit-ins would be more effective than discussions.

Even with these new ideas, the ANC did not succeed in changing apartheid. In 1959 some members broke away from the ANC and started their own group. They thought strong measures were needed to fight apartheid. This new group was called the Pan-African Congress (PAC). PAC believed that blacks should refuse to go along with the apartheid laws.

Violence at Sharpeville

The first PAC activity ended in tragedy. PAC's goal was to fight against the hated pass books. PAC members organized a protest for March 21, 1960. On that day, more than 15,000 blacks met in Sharpeville, a town southeast of Johannesburg.

The protestors gathered on the lawn outside of the Sharpeville police station. Some burned their pass books. Others waved them or threw them in the grass. They wanted to show disrespect for the

An African National Congress rally. The ANC is dedicated to fighting for the rights of blacks in South Africa.

books and for the government that forced them to carry such identification.

The police at Sharpeville decided to use force to break up the large crowd. They fired at the protestors. Thousands of people panicked and ran. The police kept firing and charged at the crowd. The police used whips, clubs, rifles, and pistols.

When the violence and shooting ended, 69 blacks lay dead on the lawn at Sharpeville. At least 178 more were wounded. Most of the victims had been shot in the back while running from the police.

The South African government was angered by the incident. It blamed PAC and the ANC for starting trouble. As a result, the government officially banned both organizations. Neither PAC nor the ANC was allowed in South Africa from that time on. In addition, the government praised the police for the way they had handled the crowd.

A Modern Hero

After the violence at Sharpeville, many blacks were angry and impatient. They felt that the peaceful methods they had been using were not effective.

One such black man was Nelson Mandela, a young leader of the banned ANC. Mandela believed it was necessary to continue fighting apartheid. The ANC went "underground"—that is, it continued its activities secretly. The ANC set up headquarters in the nearby country of Zambia.

Mandela thought that the ANC should become more aggressive. He started a military branch of the ANC, which he named

Umkhonto We Sizwe, or Spear of the Nation. Umkhonto We Sizwe began a campaign of destruction. Its goal was not to hurt people but to destroy buildings owned by whites. Power plants, fuel depots, and military bases in South Africa were bombed and set on fire.

The white government knew who was behind these acts. In 1963 Mandela was arrested and tried for sabotage. Sabotage is a secret act of destruction against the government. He was convicted and sentenced to life in prison.

Early in 1990, after 27 years, Nelson Mandela was released from prison. He is no longer a young man—he is 71 years old—and he has survived tuberculosis and other health problems. Although a man named Oliver Tambo has been running the ANC from Zambia, Nelson Mandela is still considered the leader of the group and of black South Africa.

In fact, many people think that Mandela is the one voice all black South Africans respect. A poll, or survey, taken recently among blacks found that 76 percent believed Nelson Mandela was the real leader of black South Africans. Both blacks and whites see his release from prison as a sign that the white government may be willing to discuss ending apartheid. Some are even beginning to hope peace can be worked out between blacks and whites.

28   *Nelson Mandela, recently released from prison after 27 years, is a central figure in the fight against apartheid.*

Steven Biko and "Black Consciousness"

Another respected black among South Africans was Steven Biko. He died in 1977, but even today—13 years after his death—Biko remains a powerful figure among blacks. Some refer to him as a martyr, a person willing to die for his or her beliefs. Like most martyrs, Biko has aroused great emotion in his followers.

Biko was a young man who was ready to fight apartheid. He believed, however, that the key to blacks' success in South Africa was an attitude. He called that attitude "black consciousness."

The idea behind black consciousness was pride and independence. Biko thought that whites had tried to bury the spirit and self-confidence of blacks over the years. Apartheid laws had made many blacks doubt whether they were worth anything at all. Many had given up hope—they had stopped dreaming of a better future.

Steven Biko urged blacks to assert themselves. His motto was: "Black man, you're on your own." In other words, black Africans should not wait for whites to grant them equality. They had to work hard in school, even if their schools were poor. They had to regain some of their pride and spirit. His message was similar to that of the American black civil rights leader Martin Luther King, Jr.

At first the government of South Africa was not worried about the black consciousness movement. Because they believed in nonviolence, Steven Biko and his followers were not banned like the ANC. However, in 1977 the government arrested Biko and put him in jail. They were worried that his ideas would lead to violence and more trouble in South Africa.

30

A week after he was put in prison, the government announced that Biko was dead. The police claimed that Biko had gone on a hunger strike. They said that he had refused to eat unless he was released. However, black witnesses in the jail reported that Biko had been beaten to death by the police.

Blacks all over South Africa mourned the death of Steven Biko. Today many of them regard Biko as a hero who must not be forgotten. His ideas about black pride and education are as important now as they were in 1977.

Disaster at Soweto

One tragic black consciousness effort will never be forgotten in South Africa. It happened in Soweto township in 1976.

The government decided that black students must begin taking some of their classes in the Afrikaans language. Black leaders and students were furious. They wanted to study English, as well as some of the black African languages. Afrikaans was not their language. It was the language of the hated white government. It was the language of the police. And it was the language of apartheid.

More than ten thousand students gathered at Soweto to protest the government's action. They chanted, yelled, and waved large signs. The students marched toward a stadium in Soweto. They planned to have a rally to protest the government's decision. However, the rally never took place.

The students were met by a platoon of police. The police had rifles and pistols, which they fired into the air. They also shot tear-gas canisters into the crowd. Suddenly the peaceful demonstrators

turned into a frightened mob. Police fired shots into the crowd. A young boy was killed; a woman was shot as she walked into a shop.

The scene quickly became ugly. A few blacks angrily hurled rocks at police. Helicopters dropped more tear gas on the growing crowd. Looting, burning, and shooting continued, and the violence spread to other townships. It was as if someone had opened the gates and all the frustration and anger on both sides came pouring out.

When the days of violence were over, more than eight hundred people, mostly blacks, had been killed throughout the country. Hundreds more had been arrested. To escape the killing, many hundreds more had fled across the border into nearby countries.

A State of Emergency

The government of South Africa declared a "state of emergency" after the Soweto riots. That meant that the police could arrest anyone they thought might cause trouble. Such people could be held in jail, without trial, for months.

This state of emergency is still in effect. There is so much tension that violence occurs often. Many blacks feel that the state of emergency is unfair. They think the police should not have the power to jail people without trial. According to some black leaders, many blacks have been jailed for no reason at all.

Many more blacks have been killed since the riots at Soweto. In fact, between 1984 and 1986, more than 620 blacks were killed by police. However, it is not always whites who kill blacks. Many

In 1976 a protest in the township of Soweto over the forced use of the Afrikaans language in black schools left more than eight hundred people dead.

militant blacks have threatened and killed other blacks. They threaten anyone who refuses to go along with a strike or protest. Hundreds of killings have resulted from such disputes on how to fight apartheid.

A Peaceful Bishop

But many continue to fight apartheid with peaceful means. One of the best-known fighters is Desmond Tutu. An archbishop, Tutu is the leader of the Anglican church in South Africa. He has long been fighting apartheid in nonviolent ways. He believes that peace and justice will someday win out in South Africa. Some say that Tutu is perhaps the only one who is able to mediate between the ANC, the white government, and the different black groups in the country.

Often angry at the way Tutu criticizes it, the white government has tried to punish him. For instance, when America's Columbia University wanted to give Tutu an award, the South African government took his passport away. He was unable to go to the United States without it. Columbia University solved the problem, however. It sent representatives to South Africa and had the ceremony there!

Then in 1984, Archbishop Tutu was awarded the Nobel Peace Prize—one of the greatest honors in the world. This time the government did not dare to stop him from leaving the country. Tutu was so famous, and the award so important, that the government would have looked very bad, indeed.

Tutu has risked his life several times in his long fight against racism. He once threw himself between a policeman and a gang

34   *Archbishop Desmond Tutu, the head of the Anglican church in South Africa, received the Nobel Peace Prize for his nonviolent struggle against apartheid.*

of angry blacks. Witnesses said that if Tutu had not done that, the policeman surely would have been killed.

Tutu is worried about his country. He knows that a civil war between blacks and whites is possible. However, he thinks such violence can be avoided if the white government takes apart the system of apartheid bit by bit. As for his own safety, he is not concerned. "The most awful thing that they can do," he explains, "is to kill me. And death is not the worst thing that could happen to a Christian."

SOUTH AFRICA AND THE WORLD

How does the rest of the world view South Africa? Not surprisingly, it is one of the most hated nations on earth. The reason is because of the apartheid laws.

A Nation Apart

Because South Africa's racial laws are cruel and inhumane, many countries refuse to trade with it. The nations that participate in the Olympic games refuse to let athletes from South Africa compete. And although a South African leader helped write the rules of the United Nations in 1945, the country has been barred from its seat in the General Assembly because of its apartheid policy.

This reaction from the rest of the world makes South Africa a nation apart. Some South Africans are comfortable with this role. Their ancestors, the Boers, were known for being fiercely independent and stubborn. The fact that they were on their own in the world made them proud. Critics of South Africa say that it is that Boer spirit that caused the apartheid problem to begin with. The stubbornness and lack of concern about what others think can be harmful, they say.

Sanctions

One of the ways other nations show their disapproval of South Africa's laws is by using trade sanctions. Sanctions are a policy of refusing to buy goods from or sell goods to a certain country. If South Africa cannot buy the goods it needs from other nations, it suffers. If it cannot sell the products it manufactures, it also suffers. The nations that use the sanctions hope that South Africa will suffer so much that the government will decide to change.

However, South Africa has used its independent spirit to become a "sanction buster." In other words, it has learned that it cannot rely on other countries for support or aid. It has learned, instead, to rely on itself. For instance, when the United States and other nations refused to sell weapons to South Africa, the country began to develop its own defense system. Now its military might is one of the most powerful in the world.

The same is true of some of the goods South Africa produces. Many countries of the world depend on the metals mined in South Africa. Such metals as gold, silver, chromium, and copper are important to nations that manufacture goods. Sanctions hurt those

People all over the world have shown their anger at the apartheid system by holding protests and demanding the use of trade sanctions against South Africa.

countries as well as South Africa. The government of South Africa knows that the products it mines are valuable.

The United States, as well as other Western nations such as Great Britain and West Germany, have investments in South Africa. Many of the largest companies in America have had factories and branch offices there. Ford Motor Company and General Motors had automobile assembly plants there. Kellogg's, Eastman Kodak, and IBM had factories and offices there, too. These are just a few of the American companies that were located in South Africa.

However, the United States has felt pressure to use sanctions against South Africa. There have been large demonstrations on college and university campuses. The students urged the U.S. government to impose sanctions. Many Americans think it is wrong to do business with a country in which blacks and other races cannot vote or live decently. Americans who feel this way have urged the government to pull U.S. businesses out of South Africa.

In recent years, some U.S. businesses have left South Africa. But the U.S. government has not broken off ties completely, for at least two reasons. The first reason is that American presidents have wanted to keep the lines of communication open. They say that if the United States were to refuse to have anything to do with South Africa because of apartheid, it would lose its influence there. The U.S. government would no longer be in a position to criticize, discuss, or even offer suggestions to South African officials. On the other hand, as long as America keeps polite relations with South Africa, there is always the possibility that America could help bring about change.

The other reason America has not imposed sanctions completely is out of concern for black South Africans. Many business experts have stated that the government of South Africa would be hurt very little by American sanctions. South African whites would not be hurt greatly, either. The real losers in sanctions against South Africa, say some people, would be blacks.

Blacks are the ones who do the assembly work in the factories, and the ones who mine the gold and copper. Any cutbacks in these areas would affect blacks first. And because the blacks are usually quite poor to begin with, they would surely suffer most. Whites, on the other hand, are generally more educated and possess higher skills because of this education. They could find jobs in other industries if necessary.

Archbishop Tutu disagrees with the critics of sanctions. He has stated that blacks are willing to sacrifice for long-term gains. He thinks that sanctions, if given a chance, would send a clear message to South Africa: The civilized nations of the world won't tolerate apartheid. A recent survey among South African blacks supports Tutu's opinion. More than 70 percent of blacks favor sanctions against their country, even if it would mean fewer jobs for black workers.

Slow Progress

Some South Africans say that progress has been made. They point to recent changes in apartheid laws. The law requiring blacks to carry pass books, for example, was changed in 1986. Also, it is no longer illegal for a white and a black to marry each other. Blacks now use "white" water fountains and sit on park benches that used to be marked WHITES ONLY.

Some of these changes have come about because of new laws. Many, however, came about because blacks simply ignored the old apartheid laws. The use of "white only" beaches is one example. Many of the nicest beaches have been off-limits for years to blacks. Recently, however, black families have begun showing up at the beaches. In September 1989, a crowd of eight thousand blacks visited two all-white beaches in the city of Durban. There were no demonstrations, no rallies. Police stood waiting for trouble. But except for a few white hecklers yelling insults, there was no trouble.

The same thing happened when blacks began showing up at hospitals for whites. By law white hospital workers could have turned them away. However, they were treated in the emergency rooms. "There was no fuss," said a white nurse at a Johannesburg hospital. "The people were ailing, and they were seen, same as any others. The law says we should send them to black hospitals. But those are crowded, and ours is empty. Why bother about such a thing?"

Petty Apartheid

Laws about what hospitals a black can use, or what drinking fountains, or what benches are known as petty apartheid. They are minor insults to blacks compared with the greater problem of apartheid. Changing these laws does not solve the apartheid problem.

Blacks—and a growing number of whites in South Africa— know the real issue is voting. When blacks (as well as Asians and

One example of the changes beginning to happen in South Africa is that blacks may now freely enjoy some of the areas once reserved for whites only.

coloreds) can vote and hold office, they will truly have a voice in the government.

The new president of South Africa, Frederik de Klerk, has stated that a new age is beginning in that country: "There is but one way to peace, to justice for all. That is the way of reconciliation; of together seeking mutually acceptable solutions; of together discussing what the new South Africa will look like."

Many black South Africans, including Archbishop Tutu, say they will wait and see. They would like to believe that the new government is serious about solving the problems in their troubled land. Time will tell, they say, if the changes will happen soon enough to prevent even greater violence.

FACTS ABOUT SOUTH AFRICA

Capitals: The legislative capital is Cape Town;
the administrative is Pretoria; the judicial is Bloemfontein

Population: 37 million

Form of government: A republic with a lawmaking body called
the Parliament, a state president, and a court system

Official languages: English and Afrikaans

Chief products: Asbestos, coal, diamonds, silver, gold, uranium,
copper, chemical products

Largest cities: Cape Town and Johannesburg

Glossary

apartheid *An Afrikaans word meaning "apartness." The apartheid laws, which separate the races, are what keep white South Africans in power.*

coloreds *People of mixed race, usually the descendants of black African slaves and Dutch settlers.*

homelands *Areas far from the whites in which black Africans are forced to live.*

martyr *One who suffers and dies for a cause.*

pacifist *A person opposed to violence and war.*

petty apartheid *Laws that discriminate against blacks in small, everyday ways, such as those that keep blacks from using beaches and water fountains reserved for whites.*

sabotage *A secret act of destruction against a country or government.*

sanctions *A policy of halting trade with another country.*

segregation *The separation of races.*

townships *Areas next to white towns or cities in South Africa. They are set aside for blacks who work in those cities.*

white supremacy *The belief that white people are by nature better or smarter than people of other races.*

45

Index

African National Congress (ANC) 24, 25, 26, 27, 28, 30, 34
Afrikaans 8, 31
Afrikaner 12, 14, 22
Asians 8, 12, 15, 21, 24, 25, 41

Biko, Steven 30, 31
black Africans 9, 17, 18, 19, 20, 22, 24, 28, 30, 31, 40, 43
black consciousness 30, 31
Blood River 12
Boer War 12
Boers 9, 11, 12, 14, 15, 37
British 9, 11, 12, 14

Cape of Good Hope 9
colored people 5, 6, 9, 14, 15, 25, 43
Columbia University 34

de Klerk, President Frederik 5, 43

Durban 41
Dutch 8, 9
Dutch East India Company 9

Eastman Kodak 39
Election Day 5, 6

Ford Motor Company 39

General Motors 39

Hebrews 11
Hitler 15
homelands 17, 18, 21

IBM 39
India 9

Johannesburg 18, 19, 22, 24, 25, 41

Kellogg's 39
Kimberley 12
King, Dr. Martin Luther, Jr. 30

46

Malan, Daniel 14, 15, 24
Mandela, Nelson 27, 28

National party 14, 24
Nazis 15
Nobel Peace Prize 34

Olympic games 36
Orange Free State 11

Pan-African Congress (PAC)
  25, 27
Parliament 5
pass laws 19
petty apartheid 41
Puritans 9

Race Classification Act 15

sanctions 37, 38, 39, 40
Sharpeville 25, 27
Soweto 18, 19, 31, 33

Tambo, Oliver 28
townships 6, 18, 19, 20, 31, 33

Transvaal 11
Tutu, Archbishop Desmond
  18, 34, 36, 40, 43

Umkhonto We Sizwe
  (Spear of the Nation) 28
United Nations 36

Verwoerd, Hendrik 15, 21

white supremacy 14, 15, 24

Zambia 27
Zulus 11

MAY 16 1994

J968   Stewart, Gail B.
Ste   South Africa
56145.

WITHDRAWN